The Crystal Zoo

Three Poets

General Editor: Michael Harrison

The Crystal Zoo

John Cotton
L. J. Anderson
U. A. Fanthorpe

Oxford University Press

Oxford Toronto Melbourne

Oxford University Press, Walton Street, Oxford OX2 6DP

Oxford London
New York Toronto Melbourne Auckland
Kuala Lumpur Singapore Hong Kong Tokyo
Delhi Bombay Calcutta Madras Karachi
Nairobi Dar es Salaam Cape Town

and associated companies in
Beirut Berlin Ibadan Mexico City Nicosia

Oxford is a trade mark of Oxford University Press

Three Poets
General Editor: Michael Harrison

British Library Cataloguing in Publication Data
Cotton, John, *1925-*
   The crystal zoo. (Three Poets; v. 4)
      1. Children's poetry, English
      I. Title   II. Anderson, L. J. (Lesley Jane)
      III. Fanthorpe, U. A.   IV. Harrison, Michael, *1939-*
      V. Series
      821'.914'0809282   PZ8

   ISBN 0-19-276054-8

Typeset in Great Britain by Set Fair
Printed in Great Britain by
Butler & Tanner Ltd., Frome

Contents

U. A. FANTHORPE

John Cotton

Totleigh Riddles

1   Insubstantial I can fill lives,
     Cathedrals, worlds.
     I can haunt islands,
     Raise passions
     Or calm the madness of kings.
     I've even fed the affectionate.
     I can't be touched or seen,
     But I can be noted.

2   We are a crystal zoo,
     Wielders of fortunes,
     The top of our professions.
     Like hard silver nails
     Hammered into the dark
     We made charts for mariners.

3   I reveal your secrets.
     I am your morning enemy,
     Though I give reassurance of presence
     I can be magic,
     Or the judge in beauty contests.
     Count Dracula has no use for me.
     When you leave
     I am left to my own reflections.

4   My tensions and pressures
     Are precise if transitory.
     Iridescent, I can float
     And catch small rainbows,
     Beauties luxuriate in me.
     I can inhabit ovens
     Or sparkle in bottles.
     I am filled with that
     Which surrounds me.

5   Containing nothing
     I can bind people for ever,
     Or just hold a finger.
     Without end or beginning
     I go on to appear in fields,
     Ensnare enemies,
     Or in another guise
     Carry in the air
     Messages from tower to tower.

6   Silent I invade cities,
     Blur edges, confuse travellers,
     My thumb smudging the light.
     I drift from rivers
     To loiter in early morning fields,
     Until constable sun
     Moves me on.

7   Rain polishes
     My round the year gloss,
     Honing my row
     Of sharp spears.
     In winter I come into my own,
     Bearing the crown
     And gifts
     Of bright beads of blood.

8   I work while you sleep,
Needing no light to etch windows
Or elaborate leaf or branch.
Without colour my wonder is
My patterns within patterns
Growing like crisp stars.
Look, but do not touch.
Your warmth is my end.

9   A great cold cinder,
At year's end I face the sun
Across pale-washed skies,
Outshone but not outpulled.
Ruling tides, blood and calendars,
I float on water, bend minds,
And like knowledge
Illumine but not warm.

10   I am one of an endless family,
My brothers and sisters
Never far behind.
I crash and swirl,
Grind pebbles, growl,
And gnaw the bones of the land
Like a great wet dog.

11   Painted or plain,
Of earth or glass,
Being filled
My purpose is fulfilled.
Water or wine
My being is in holding,
Though I, too, am held
By my unhearing ear.

12 My momentary delights
    Are held close
    In a paper bud,
    I flower best at night,
    My petals falling
    Like bright showers
    When I am fired to beauty.

Answers on page 19

Listen

Silence is when you can hear things.
Listen:
The breathing of bees,
A moth's footfall,
Or the mist easing its way
Across the field,
The light shifting at dawn
Or the stars clicking into place
At evening.

In the Kitchen

In the Kitchen,
After the aimless
Chatter of the plates,
The murmurings of the gas,
The chuckle of the water pipes
And the sharp exchanges
Of knives, forks and spoons,
Comes the serious quiet,
When the sink slowly clears its throat
And you can hear the occasional rumble
Of the refrigerator's tummy
As it digests the cold.

Moorland Signals

Behind the stone cottage
the wife pegs out her washing,
a bright bunting
of challenge to the grey
power of the moor
which, like the vasts
of a terrestrial sea, casts
up, from time to time,
a pony or a sheep.
Out of the mists and rime
such visitors stare at night
at the homing beacon
of the cottage's square of light.

Horse Chestnuts

Autumn's special toys,
There is something about the newness of them,
Their gloss, the colour of burnished horses,
Their richness protected from their fall
By those thick green cases,
So that we can harvest them
Safe in their nests
Of last year's debris of leaves,
To pocket them
For treasure or for play.
Though they will never be
Quite so beautiful again,
As that first moment
When we saw them peep pristine
From their soft-spiked shells.

Allotments

Here, where the best crop is stones,
between the churchyard and the railway,
are the allotments, divided
by grass strips, where turnips, white,
hard, round, compete with pebbles,
sparse cabbage struggles towards spring,
and plastic, like prayer flags,
scares birds from half planted rows
as regular as rails.
All this care for so little.

The churchyard grows its stones too,
each plot well marked: 'In Loving
Memory' or 'Safe with Jesus',
sparrows darting amongst them –
a fresh one gaudy with tributes,
and one, neglected, small, for
Thomas Jeremy aged three,
its metal urn rust eaten –
the knapped flint of the church,
close by, still growing.

Bracken

Vegetable phoenix,
the bracken, out of the dry
combustible debris of
their predecessors, thrust up
green hoops, later to straighten
as they push towards the sun.
The young fronds tight and foetus-
like, each pair's slow unfolding
(measurable only by days)
maintains an exact balance
until the delicately
feathered leaf-wings are fully
extended to hover like birds.
Heath fires can set bracken back,
not destroy them. Cut them back
or attempt to suppress them,
as with thoughts or emotions,
they will reappear. Their reserves
are deeper. Similarly,
note how once they take a hold
little else flourishes.
Stand still a moment, can't you
feel them pushing, pushing
to the surface?

Autumnal

Free from the screeching night omens
Of owls, I walk alone the length
Of this oozing autumn morning,
The grasses mist drenched, the briars rich
In the congealed gouts of their hips.
Feet squelch in the soft rot of leaves
Where, in the cold aisles of the trees,
Fungi construct out of the mould
Their unlit, ephemeral selves.

Approaching the trees, cathedral
Branched, their great trunks isolated
In mist heavy with the incense
Of decay, I touch their dark, moss
Dank bark to know them in their fall,
Leaf scars sealed, locked in essential
Loneliness against that season
When tenacity is all, and
To each its own preparation.

Camping

Once a year we would go to camp,
Humping our kitbags to where
The lorry would take them off to Devon.
Then by train and coach we sped away from town
To a field where the moors rolled away like the sea,
The woods were as dark as caves
And the spring water tasted sharp as a knife.
We heaved the heavy canvas of bell-tents upon their
     poles,
To which our feet would point at night
As we lay in our blankets like spokes in a wheel.
And the youngest of us would wake long before the
     others.
Lying still and watching, through the triangle of
     doorway,
The shifting light of dawn, the mist dispersing,
And listening to the mysterious dry-throated call of the
     distant wood-pigeons,
We felt alone and strangers in a world
Where the true citizens were the ponies and sheep in the
     fields close by,
Yet sensing, for all that,
That we had returned to what was ours.

The Wilderness

'This is the wilderness,' my uncle said:
A corner of the garden he'd let go,
Grass waist high and trees grown spindly
Because they were too close together,
A contrast to the rose beds, well mown lawn
And ranks of vegetables. There we would play
Where Indians, outlaws and rugged pioneers
Haunted the patch of wonder surviving
In a suburb. It's all gone now: childhood, uncle,
The patch sold to more determined gardeners.
To remember is to miss that place
Where imagination grew, lost now
In the cautious cultivation of our days.
'All gardens should have one,' uncle said.
We should have listened to him.

Torches

It is the torches I remember best.
Going home on a winter's evening
We would point them skyward,
Screwing the fronts to sharpen the pencils of light
That they might pierce the darkness the better.
Bold young challengers of stars,
We competed in length and brightness.
Yes, better than the chips,
Tart with vinegar and salt grains,
In bags like small grease-proof hats,
Better even than the large orange bottles,
Tizer tasting of fruit that never was,
Were the torches,
Their beams like friendly knives
Making cuts in a darkness
Which oh so quickly healed
At the touch of a switch.

Visiting

The room in my head is full of people.
My mother talks and they appear:
Uncles, aunts, a splendid cousin,
Some gone, some long unremembered, they're all
    there.
Yet the mirror reflects but the two of us,
The four walls containing only their box of air,
While uncle laughs and aunts pour tea.
Their spirit lives while we remember them.

Answers to Totleigh Riddles

1. Music	7.	Holly
2. Stars	8.	Frost
3. Mirror	9.	Moon
4. Bubbles	10.	Wave
5. Ring	11.	Jug
6. Fog	12.	Firework

L. J. Anderson

Birth

First the seed, bearing in a speck
The insect mask on the lip of the orchid,
The marquetry of the drake's feathers,
The stripes of the lemur and the eland,
The mackerel and the tabby cat:
Then growth of the folded form –
Wing and bone and heart and fin and finger:
Then the fern-head impelled through stony ground,
The unfledged bird battering at the shell,
The voyage of the human child through unyielding
    flesh:
Then the moment of light,
Full of hope, full of terror.

The Vision Scene

The chaffinches were feeding on the spindleberries;
I heard them flitting and piping
As we played at blind-man's buff
On the terrace beyond the hornbeam alley.
The countess, my mother,
Watched from a velvet stool
And servants busied themselves with silver kettles
In the pavilion.

Beyond the paling, in the flat of the park
I saw the blue mountain, invisible
To them, and yet to me so real
That I smelled the chill of the wooded slopes,
Felt the dust of a hundred years on the thorn hedge
With its bitter sloes.
Under the north wall, a sapling ash tree
Cast its leaves in the long wet grass.
The silence of the courtyard
Was more like a death than a sleep,
But high above me
The late sun shone like a beacon
On the window of the chamber in the tower.

The Twelve Princesses

The night is what we live for,
When the bed sinks through the floor
And we drift down the steps to the lake
Where the twelve boats are waiting.
The water is warm through our trailing fingers,
Luminous, aquamarine.
The wind comes soft and scented with moon-flowers.
On the further shore
We walk through groves of gold and silver branches
Gleaming in that cool blue light
That is neither day nor darkness.
And then in a clearing we come to the dancing floor.
Ah – the bliss of that dancing
In that open place
Under that dome of dim yet lucent blue.
Our hair is loose, our shifts are unconstraining,
Our slippered feet skim across the ground
And the one firm thing
Is the arms of the strong young princes.
They are all alike, all beautiful;
They smile at us; we do not know their names.
How terrible the day is –
The waking, the effort,
Heavy bodies in heavy clothes,
The men's faces quirky, irregular,
The noise, the draughts, the stairs.
Listless, we hide our worn-out slippers
And wait for night.

On the Way to the Sleeping Beauty

It was all quite different on the third day:
There were clearings
Where sun dappled the grass –
That emerald dew-webbed autumn grass
That looks like the floor of another world.
The blue hills seen through the trees
Seemed to borrow magic,
As if the air in those golden branches
Was no ordinary air.
All day long I heard the hunt in the distance,
Saw in my mind's eye the joy of the scarlet and green,
Heard the hounds with pleasure still,
Though I knew I should not meet them now.
As I moved through that sunlit country
Other worlds marched with mine,
Half remembered, it seemed to me, half guessed at.
I was alone, yet not alone,
Not feeling her presence, yet knowing now
At each dividing of the ways I should choose rightly.
Then suddenly at evening, there was the castle
In the splendour of its black-laced trees,
The leaves of its poplars fluttering like banners,
Travelling geese flying over, high in the bright sky,
And I knew that deep in the sleeping heart of it
Lay the new beginning.

Beauty and the Beast

A merchant, returning, remembered the gift for his
    daughter,
Picked a rose from the hedge that circled my lands,
A red rose, a token,

And so fell in my power, the evil that held me,
And as gage for his life, sent me his best-loved treasure,
His white rose, his Beauty,

To be my unwilling guest. But so great was her longing
That I let her return for a month and a day,
My white rose, my beauty.

But once she was there, she forgot her promise,
Forgot her duty to me, her ugly lord,
My white rose, my captive.

The cold power of the spell and the betrayal,
The force of the broken vow broke me with grief
For my white rose, my love,

Till she, seeking her face in the glass, saw my deathbed,
Knew what she had done, flew to my side without
    thinking
And I rose from my bed a prince, a man transformed
By my red rose, my love.

Sleeping Beauty

I pushed ajar the little door in the wall;
The blue stone of the kitchen yard
Was strewn with wet fig leaves.
In I walked
Through a scullery.
On the slab
I saw a cracked dish of quinces;
Their scent was thin, yet strong
And spicy cold.
On the table in the great kitchen
Lay pale sheaves of celery;
A white cloth, twisted,
Had fallen on the floor.
The air was drier
In the panelled hall,
Warmer, faintly scented with sandalwood.
A ray of late sun
Struck a brocaded chair.
The banister was chill
As I put my foot
On the first step
Of the great stair.

Cold, in the old barn,
Dark too, with the one lantern,
Not much colour.
Caked mud on the purple roots in the corner;
Slashes pale in the willow hurdles;
Dry as old parchment,
A tangle of bleached horms
Hangs with a halter from a nail.
Dust falls from the matted ivy
As the pigeons clatter
To roost in the dark of the beams.
I think then of the weary family,
Travel-stained and numb,
Camped in the lantern's circle
On the stamped-earth floor,
Bounded by bundled rushes,
Splintery logs and sacks of meal
On the night when the lion
Ate straw like the ox
And the wolf dwelled with the lamb.

The Boy Who Was Taken by the Snow Queen

No no no, you are wrong to pity me,
For I have seen such wonders
In my time in the land of snow and ice.
I have stood on the topmost tower
As they reeled out the northern lights across the sky
Like bolts of shot silk.
I have sat in the high-ribbed hall
At the foot of the white throne
Flanked by two swathing spear-bones
From the cheek of a great fish.
I have seen how the plant soul abroad in the air
Is materialized for our delight
In ferns on the window-pane,
How the swirl and flow of the living stream
Is charted in lines of ice
And the secrets of the crystal world
Are tossed to us in a million million snowflakes.
I have seen how they transmute
The freezing vapours of a winter's night
To the hoar frost's white fires,
So men can wake to see with new eyes
Each twig, each crust, each cabbage leaf.
No, do not pity me,
For I have sat in a blaze of white light
In the cave at the heart of winter;
It is you who are in the dark.

Cinderella at the Ball

Though my sisters were there, I half believed
It was a fairy place of her creating,
A place out of time, where spring and summer
Were conjured to the depths of winter.
As my carriage drew up, the scent of hidden flowers
Came from the dark of the snow-bound garden
And pollen drifted down from strange grey catkins
In the lights from the ballroom windows.
The lines of the rooms swirled;
Space became a partner in the dance
And glass reflecting glass
Opened vistas of infinite possibility
Down which the mind reeled.
Marble floors and pillars shone
With the crocus flames of the candles,
Speckled marble, flowered marble,
Marble veined like cheese,
Marble with a world in its depths
Like the brawn on our pantry shelves.
On the sideboards lay fish like psalters,
Dishes of bright fruits
Sliced across their jewelled secrets,
Fruit whose rough cases
Were flushed with exquisite pink,
Heart-shaped fruit with heart-shaped scales
Like an angel's folded wings.
There were flowers in porcelain baskets,
The eye green, frilled with strange colours –
Dark red of marbled beef,
Mealy white, indigo, beeswax yellow,
The milky green of young oats,
Purplish black like steeping walnuts,
Colours I never expected to see in flowers.

But then everything,
Everything was unexpected.
My sisters were touched by it, I think;
They came home satisfied,
Yet subdued, as if they had seen something,
But did not understand it, did not really want to.
They were not, as I was,
Utterly changed.

Green Epiphany

By the thirteenth day
The wind came from a new quarter.
I went out in the mild green morning
And sat on a sack by the ruined wall.
Beyond it grew a tree,
A little tree,
With crab-apples crimson as cherries.
A few lay fallen by the wall
With the bones of some small animal.
Meagre but resilient, the jasmine
Had put out starry sprays from a pile of rubble.
A carpet of dark green leaves
Brushed at my skirt.
It was the periwinkle,
Here and there a flower;
Too tender it seemed,
That hot sweet blue, for winter.
On the eaves the ring-doves fluted and clattered.
The child
Fingered a wooden spoon.
Inside the stable door, the dusty sun
Shone on the casket of myrrh.

The Kiss

One kiss
And the hundred-year sleep of the spindle is ended.
The circling thicket that guarded the spell-death
With tangles and brambles and maces of thorn
Is quickened with budding, transformed in a twinkling,
Burgeoning, breaking with tendrils, awakening.
The air is moist and scented with ferns.
Through the black alders
Shine lights from the castle across open water
And the birds still sing when it's too dark to see.

Godiva

The worst was the beginning.
I came down the stair and out into the court;
One of my women, with averted eyes, held the bridle.
The other, as I took off my cloak,
Cupped her hand for my bare foot
And we struggled, for the horse's flank was slippery
And part of my shame was a horse without saddle
Such as only the poorest ride.
I did not look at them again, but I heard them weeping
As I rode out under the arch.
The horse seemed somehow a stranger
As I felt his animal sinews moving under me.
The streets were empty
But I could not believe I was alone

And as I thought of the eyes on me
My body seemed to burn.
All the unfamiliar sensations added to my confusion –
The purposeful rhythmn of the cob's muscles,
The wind, which was cool, yet strangely pleasing,
A blossom, blown from a tree,
Hitting me with a tiny sting,
Then a flurry of rain –
Hard, precise and yet unknowing drops.
When at last I returned from the town,
The courtyard seemed the more menacing
Because it had known my first distress.
Refusing the proffered cloak,
I walked in as I was, to find him.
He would not look at me,
But I was no longer ashamed.
Obscurely I sensed I had won more
Than a lowering of taxes.

The swallows reel across the sky like kites
And hearing them,
Seeing the first blue iris
And stone plants creeping
In the pebbles by the path,
The nomad heart
Leaps the garden wall,
Passes the town gate swiftly
And travels out on the wide plain,
The track that leads
To distant and invisible mountains,
Pausing in its flight
By a fringed pool
Where the caked mud is marked
By the trampling of hooves.

Michaelmas

The cold tightens round my heart
At the fading of the light;
The chill comes up from the dank nettles,
The rank elder and the autumn grass;
Fear of the dying of the year
And the long winter's night.

The ground trembles under my feet
As if at the advance
Of the legions of evil;
The black road shimmers, but not with heat.
Then out of the west, into the world's dark wood
Rides Michael with his lance.

U. A. Fanthorpe

Riddle

Awash in the watery airway, I drift
But never stray from my moorings.

Child of a year, I am born
In the spray, fade in the fall.

My submissive brethren wait man's time;
I create my own moment,

Leaning from my twiggy rigging
Into the wind's hand, finding

A mutineer's grave in my grassy landfall.
Wasps are my monument.

Answer on page 48

Supermarket Thought

The kestrel's wide-fanned tail
    And nervous claws
Reflect the shrew's spread ears
    And helpless paws.

The prey defines its predator.
    We are the neat,
Drugged, frozen, graceless packages
    We eat.

The Butcher's Cat

The scuffled blood-stains on the sawdust floor
Dripped from the patient necks of pigs, who hung
White-skinned, like banners. Hares swayed by the door
And little jars to catch their ooze were slung
Like muzzles to their noses. Grained and chipped
With bones and knives, the butcher's chopping board
Imperviously drank whatever dripped.
And was the tally where all cuts were scored.

Butchers are gentler now. Their windows frame
Tasteful arrangements done in shades of red.
Pale tripe, pink mince, bronze kidneys, mildly claim
Affinities with some suburban bed
Of well-groomed wallflowers. But the butcher's cat
Still licks her chops, and still looks rather fat.

Boarding Kennels

Here we lodge love when it grows inconvenient.

Here behind bars it will wait for us
While we
Go away for the week-end,
Or run up to London
For a round of theatres,
Or fly off on our summer holidays,
Or pursue any other occupation
Where love gets in the way.

Love will wait till we get back
(Being behind bars, it hasn't much choice).
It will be fed, exercised, kept
Warm, preserved from all the dangers
Incident upon being loved and being
Free. In fact, when we see it again, love
Will have put on weight. When it sees us
Love will leap in such an agony
Of joy as to spoil completely, in retrospect,
All the pleasure that we had on holiday
Without it.

Autumn Term

Now the unmanageable summer is over
Now the flow of postcards from Greece is drying up
Now male motorists no longer strip to the waist
Now gardens of riverside pubs are empty
Now friends have no more slides to show us
Now Promenaders have cheered their last piano
     concerto

Now lollipop ladies again terrorise highways
Now trees are browner and grass is greener
Now hyacinth bulbs are back in Woolworth's
Now suburban beds are stuffed with next year's
     wallflowers
Now hoses are reinterred ceremonially, like pets,
Now gangs of finches hijack hedgerows

Now we are almost at the end of the endless Sundays-
     after-Trinity
We can abandon the pretence that we enjoy summer,
When we never really feel equal to its demands.
Now we can settle down to slog through winter
Which suits our nationally wry disposition much better,
Now the swallows have gone.

Kipling Mishandled
or
A Clerical Canticle

Lo, we are the ones who uncover
  The things you'd prefer to keep dark—
Your date-of-birth, income, religion—
  For this is the power of the clerk
(Check his figures!)
  For this is the right of the clerk.

You must fill in the forms that we send you
  (And cut out that witty remark!)
Then we number you, file you and code you,
  For such is the way of the clerk
(Use the date-stamp!)
  For such is the rule of the clerk.

If you fill in our forms incorrectly
  Then the Law, which must bite when we bark,
Will prosecute quickly and fiercely,
  So it's best to come clean with a clerk
(Pass the Tipp-Ex!)
  You must tell the whole truth to a clerk.

If you query our right of intrusion,
  Our lineage goes back to the Ark,
For how could they stow all that dunnage
  Unless Shem or Ham was a clerk
(Double entry!)
  Old Noah, he needed a clerk.

For ourselves, we are sworn to keep silence.
    Even dates can betray. 'As postmark'
Is a formula *we* have found handy,
    But you can't play that trick on a clerk
(Ref'rence number!)
    Don't you try any tricks on a clerk.

When you've told us your innermost secrets,
    And we see you divested and stark,
Don't expect any patience or pity,
    For that's not the sphere of the clerk
(Time for tea-break!)
    You won't get much rope from a clerk.

For we are the Masters of Chaos,
    And nothing we do is a lark.
You bring us disorder; we tame it,
    Wherein lies the craft of the clerk
(Please turn over!)
    Law and order depend on the clerk.

On the day of the Great Registration,
    At the Last Trumpet's terrible bark,
The Angel of Records will save us,
    For he's one of *us*. He's a clerk
(Holy Orders!)
    High Heaven Itself needs a clerk.

Chinky

Staff Nurse is short and smart. Her mouth of teeth
Shines briskly like a uniform. She came,
Qualified help, to tell me what to do.

Chinky, female, four foot and Mongoloid,
Strayed from the next-door mental hospital,
And cropped up in our car-park, trying to make
Our sane cars as defective as herself,
Plucking at windscreen-wipers like harp strings.

Sent to protect the *status quo*, I found
The stolid cars looked calm, while Chinky laughed
Into their windscreens. So I parked there too.
It seemed a good enough relationship—
Six cars, a laughing daftie, and myself
To give the flawed perspective of the sane.

Staff Nurse arrived to diagnose the scene,
Prescribed a spot of body contact, put
A cautious arm round Chinky, said, *Now love,
Leave that alone.* And Chinky flung herself,
Laughing her empty head off, to the ground,
And lay there in the oily patches, laughing.

We studied her for ages, wondering
How strong she was, how mad she was, and why
She laughed. And Staff Nurse said to me,
See, love, I never did my mental training.

At last two student nurses from next door,
Big cheerful girls, removed our foreign body.
They picked an arm apiece out of the oil,
And little Chinky rose into the air,
Her simple feet dangling beside their thighs.
They laughed and she laughed. Staff Nurse said again,
See, love, I never did my mental training.

Introducing . . .

This little man
Five foot one in his socks
Is: a killer.

These burly chaps
Eyeing the little man:
Prison warders.

This starchy girl,
Professional with pill
And medicine glass,

Watching the man
As painfully he drinks,
Swallows and drinks

And gets it down,
The necessary pill,
Is: a Sister.

The pill he takes,
The big pink pill, is: for
Travel sickness.

The travel he
Needs it for: his journey
Back to prison.

The distance he
Will cover on the way
Is: three whole miles.

The pill he takes
So seriously is:
A placebo.

And we who watch
Straight-faced and intent are:
Part of the joke.

Transitional Object

Sits, holding nurse's hard reassuring hand
In her own two small ones.

Is terrified. Mews in her supersonic
Panic voice: *Help. Help. Please.*

Cries for Mummy, Daddy, Philip, the bus. Tries
To get up, to escape.

Is restrained by adult, would-be comforting
Hands and arms. Fights them.

Is brought a sweet warm drink, and is too shaky
With fear to swallow it.

The nurse cuddles her, snuggles the young amber
Ringlets against the grey.

Is not to be consoled. Her only comfort
The white blanket she hugs.

Whispers, *Help. Help. Please.* Cries for Mummy,
    Daddy,
Philip. She is 83,

Resisting childhood as it closes in.

I Do Know How Awful I Am

I have two of me.
Constantly they betray me.

One, the old gipsy,
Brown, wrinkled, with white eyelids,

Who laughs her way out
Of tight corners, holds fortune

Between her fingers,
Spits luckily on highways,

Coerces hazels,
Has no birth certificate.

This old wretch cons me,
Promises her favours,

But sends her daughter,
Pale, suburban and speechless,

Limp autumn crocus,
Whose magic is exhausted.

Naturally, when
I need such mild company,

The deplorable
Witch, her mother, comes instead.

I Can Quite Understand It

(On a picture in Bristol Art Gallery entitled: 'Boy
showing the way to an itinerant vendor of teawhisks'.)

I can quite understand it.

If anyone has devoted so much
Ingenuity to the question of
Correct choice of career as to
Come up with a solution like
Itinerant vendor of teawhisks,
Then it's clear that he won't
Have much energy left over
For more mundane employments like
Finding the way from one place
To another.

And the boy seems to be having
Some problem in helping him.

Look, mate!
Put down those blessed teawhisks and *listen*
To what the lad is saying.

My Lion is a Unicorn

My lion is a unicorn.
He, sunbrowed and splendid,
Distributes love with lavish
Paws and growls goldenly.
She, tenderhoofed and weighed
Down with incongruous
Ivory lumber, shivers
With nerves, and is
Scared of virgins.

My lion is as strong as a
Ten–ton–truck. He tosses
Pancakes and cabers with his
Debonair tail. But my
Unicorn suffers from
Cold sores, hay fever and
A weak back, not to mention
Chilblains on the sensitive
Tip of her horn.

My lion is as hot as a
Boiling kettle. He hugs
Me to his royal mane and
Comforts me. But my sad
Unicorn creeps into
My bed and whimpers, *Please
Make me happy please make me
Happy*. Darling unicorn,
You need my lion
To comfort you.

The Horse Speaks

No, not a speaking part this time,
But those are my hoofs you can hear
Four-in-a-bar-ing away. They missed
A chance to cheer up the back rows,
Not giving me a cue for a whinny,
But composers are always stingy
Over cadenzas. To be perfectly frank,
This boot-saddle-to-horse stuff
Never appeals to me much. I prefer
The peaceful world of the slow movement,
With grass in it. But even there
Sensational elements will intrude – cuckoos,
Thunderstorms, larks ascending. They can't
Leave well alone. In the present case,
Imagine me at my most statuesque,
Quietly nodding over a moonlit nosebag,
Dreaming of non-achievement. In bursts the Hero,
Inflicts saddle, bridle, spurs and purpose,
Helter-skelters into a spiteful landscape
Of black wire and barbed hedges. The moon, of course,
Goes down at once. And Heroes
Always ride cross-country.
                              The end?
Oh, the Hero gets there, naturally.
So presumably the horse does too,
In an interestingly exhausted condition.
Where? Funny you should ask me that.
I forget where we were going;
I always did confuse Ghent with Aix.

The Heir

It was very quiet on the island after
They all went back to Milan. Sounds
And sweet airs dwindled and petered out
As the fleet dissolved on Ariel's calm sea.

Caliban missed the music, being
A susceptible monster. The whole island
Was his now, sun, moon and yellow sands,
Filberts and freshets, but somehow

Vacant, and not worth having. Twangling
Instruments and spiteful hedgehogs
In retrospect mingled. He didn't know
Exactly what he was missing,

But he missed it. Prospero, he thought,
Had shipped harmony with the baggage
Back to Milan. Poor mooncalf, he didn't realise
They had all gone back to invest

In Olivetti and Neapolitan
Ice cream, abandoning magic
And music together. Only Ariel
Went on playing for love, and he never

Touched down on the island again.
His memories were quite distinct, and all
Of tyranny. So the island was soundless, airless,
Dumb to name Caliban king.

Answer to Riddle: Windfall